An Invitation to the Ball

Adapted by Andrea Posner-Sanchez

Illustrated by the Disney Storybook Artists

Random House 🏠 New York

Copyright © 2012 Disney Enterprises, Inc. All rights reserved. Published in the United States by Random House Children's Books, a division of Random House, Inc., 1745 Broadway, New York, NY 10019, and in Canada by Random House of Canada Limited, Toronto, in conjunction with Disney Enterprises, Inc. Random House and the colophon are registered trademarks of Random House, Inc.

ISBN: 978-0-7364-2897-2

randomhouse.com/kids

MANUFACTURED IN CHINA

10 9 8 7 6 5 4 3 2 1

Cinderella never stopped hoping and dreaming. Even though she was treated poorly by her mean Stepmother and stepsisters, Anastasia and Drizella, she knew that someday her dream of happiness would come true.

One day, a royal messenger arrived with an invitation to a ball. The King was inviting all the young women of the kingdom to attend. He hoped to find a bride for the Prince.

Cinderella's stepsisters were very excited to attend the royal ball! When Cinderella asked if she could go, too, her Stepmother sneered. She agreed to let Cinderella attend only if she finished all her chores and found something suitable to wear.

In her room, Cinderella found an old dress that had belonged to her mother. With some work, she could make it look like new—but she had so many chores to do! There was no time to fix the dress.

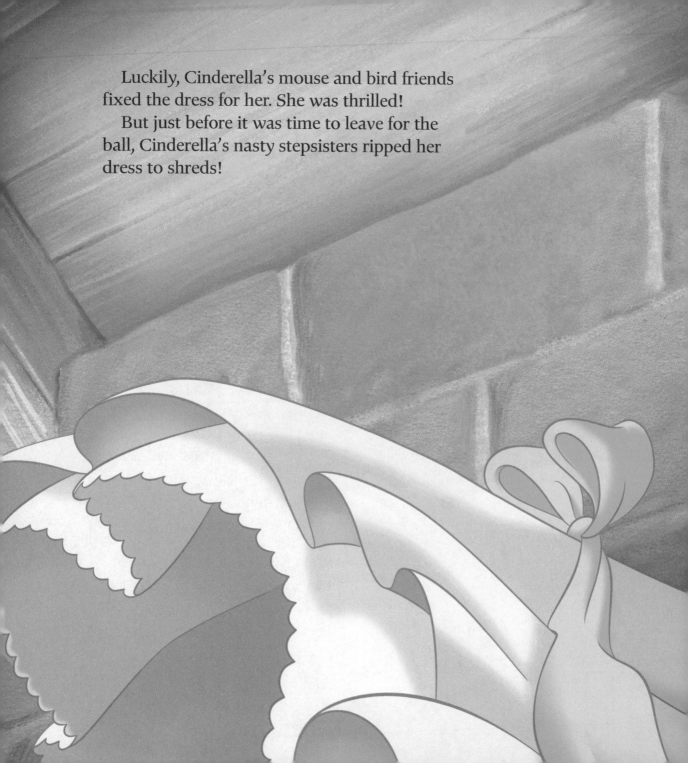

Luckily, Cinderella's mouse and bird friends fixed the dress for her. She was thrilled!

But just before it was time to leave for the ball, Cinderella's nasty stepsisters ripped her dress to shreds!

Crying, Cinderella ran outside. She had never felt so hopeless.
Suddenly, her fairy godmother appeared! With a few waves
of her magic wand, she turned a pumpkin into a coach and the
mice into coachmen. She even transformed Cinderella's torn
dress into a fancy gown and dainty glass slippers.

As soon as Cinderella entered the ballroom, the Prince rushed over to greet her. She was the most beautiful girl he had ever seen!

Cinderella spent hours with the
Prince. They danced and talked and
strolled outside in the moonlight. It
was a magical evening that Cinderella
would never forget!

© Disney
© Disney
© Disney
© Disney
© Disney
© Disney
© Disney
© Disney
© Disney
© Disney
© Disney
© Disney
© Disney
© Disney
© Disney
© Disney
© Disney
© Disney
© Disney
© Disney

© Disney

© Disney

© Disney

© Disney

© Disney

© Disney

© Disney

© Disney

© Disney

© Disney

© Disney

© Disney

Cinderella's dreams finally came true. She married her Prince, and they lived happily ever after!

Thankfully, Cinderella still had the other slipper in her pocket. The Grand Duke placed it on Cinderella's foot and announced that it was a perfect fit!

Just as the Grand Duke was about to leave, Cinderella appeared at the top of the stairs. But before she could try on the glass slipper, her nasty Stepmother tripped the footman—and the slipper shattered!

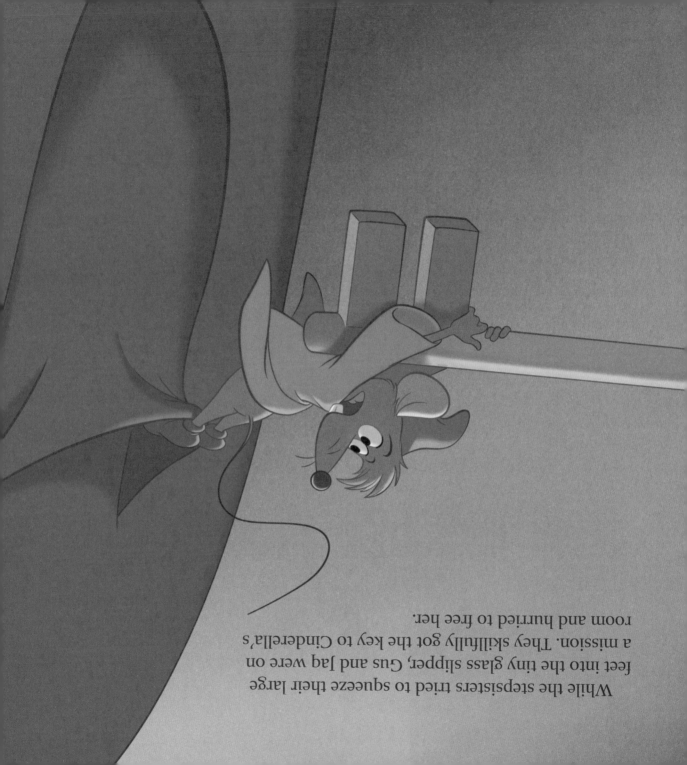

While the stepsisters tried to squeeze their large feet into the tiny glass slipper, Gus and Jaq were on a mission. They skillfully got the key to Cinderella's room and hurried to free her.

When the Grand Duke arrived at the house,
Cinderella's stepsisters greeted him happily. They
hoped to trick him into thinking one of them was
the girl the Prince was looking for.

The next day, an announcement came from the palace that the Prince wanted to marry the girl whose foot fit into the glass slipper left behind at the ball. Cinderella's Stepmother quickly realized that Cinderella was the lucky girl. She locked Cinderella in the attic room so the Prince couldn't find her.

Soon the Fairy Godmother's magical spell wore off.
The coach turned into a pumpkin, and Cinderella was
once again in her torn dress with her animal friends.
But one magical item remained—she still had the
other glass slipper.

Cinderella was having such a great time at the ball, she almost forgot that the magic would end at midnight! As the clock struck twelve, Cinderella dashed out of the palace, accidentally dropping one of her glass slippers.

The Next Princess

Adapted by Andrea Posner-Sanchez

Illustrated by the Disney Storybook Artists

Random House 🏠 New York

ISBN: 978-0-7364-2897-2

randomhouse.com/kids

MANUFACTURED IN CHINA

10 9 8 7 6 5 4 3 2 1